Plant kindness
and gather love.

- Proverb

May we always remember
that kindness
is the best gift we leave behind.

Measure Your Day in
Kindness

By Elaheh Bos

You could measure your day in food.

Taste your way through
savoury treats, or sweets.

You could mark the moment
when you'd discovered
the perfect ingredient,
eaten your weight in cheese,
created a new recipe,
or added so much salt
it could fill the seas.

You could measure your day in jumps.

Count how many times you leapt,
skipped, hopped,
sprung, or bounced.

Perhaps you jumped so high,
that for a moment you knew
that you flew.

You could measure your day in play.

In hide and seek, and hopscotch,
capture the flag, tag, marbles,
jump rope, and all the games
you would invent along the way.

In search of fun and adventure,
you could simply play the day away.

You could measure your day in nature.

In collecting leaves,
hugging trees,
and smelling flowers.

You could spend the day
lying next to a brook,
watching the water flow,
or listening to the wind blow.

Wouldn't that be quite the show?

You could measure your day in time.

Counting the seconds,
minutes, hours, days, weeks,
and years as if it were nothing more
than a sum of tics and tocks.

You could spend the day
trying to understand time
—only to realize after all
that counting and measuring—
that time flies.

You could measure your day in books.

Smiling at how many pages you read,
and how many times
your stories twisted and turned.

You could spend the entire day
marvelling at how many worlds
you visited in your book,
from the simple comfort
of your reading nook.

You could measure your day
by the company of cats.

Counting the furry tails,
the cuddles and snuggles.

You could appreciate
the simple pleasure of being
together.

You could measure your day in silence.

In that quiet solitude,
you could treasure each yawn
as you stretched your body out long.

Some days call for nothing,
so you could spend the day
lazing away,
filling up for the next day,
and remembering
that all would be okay.

You could measure your day in song.

Each chord telling a story,
each word rhyming away
to the music's sway.

You could sing to your heart's delight,
and your joy for the song
would make everyone want to sing along.

You could measure your day
in knowledge.

Memorizing facts
or creating new formulas.

You could dissect plants, observe insects,
and spend the day learning new ways
to understand the world.

A day spent discovering something new
could be the best of days.

You could measure your day in inventions.

You could create flying machines,
floating monkeys,
fabulous magnets,
and be the most fearsome maker.

And while you crafted away,
new ideas would simply
float your way.

You could measure your day in art.

In brush patterns, and paint swatches.

You could draw, paint, sketch,
collage, or doodle the day away.

The colours would whisper to you,
turquoise, lavender, periwinkle,
crimson, pewter, cream,
all nudging you to look their way,
all asking to become alive
with their colorful sway.

You could do all that and more...

And each day would be magical
in its own way.

But what if you measured
your day in kindness?

You would see that kindness
lives on, kindness grows.

Kindness creates more kindness,
and kindness flows.

Kindness brings people together.

Kindness makes hearts float.

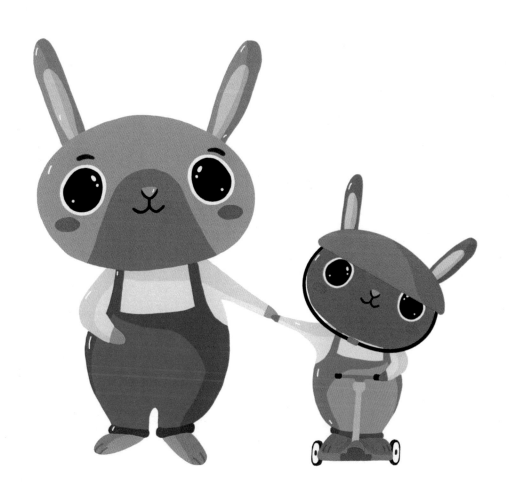

And should your day be long,
or should your day be short,
if measured in kindness,
it would be a day
that glows and grows.

You could measure your day in hugs,
in cuddles, in smooches,
and in smiles.

Kindness leaves a mark.
Kindness leaves a heart print.

You could measure your day
in togetherness.

You could measure your day
in gratitude,
and filling your heart
with a blessing each day.

You could measure your day
in sharing what you love,
in patiently showing the way,
in kind deeds, in acts of service,
in scoops of helping,
in listening, and caring.

And if you did,
wouldn't that be
the most beautiful way
to measure a day?

Let's talk about kindness!

"Plant kindness and gather love."

– Proverb

Think about this proverb and what it means.
What other things might grow when we plant seeds of kindness?

Here are some ways to explain kindness.

Kindness:
The quality of being friendly, generous, and considerate.

Kindness means caring and doing nice deeds for others. We are kind when we take care of animals and other people, as well as do our best to make others happy through our actions. You can show kindness in many different ways. Saying something nice or doing something to help someone are nice ways to show kindness.

Can you think of other ways to explain kindness?

_____

_____

_____

_____

Kindness is important because:

- Being kind makes us feel good.
- Kindness is contagious in a good way.
- Kindness builds bridges and communities.
- Kindness helps us when we are feeling down.
- Kindness can help brighten someone's day.
- Being kind reminds us that we all matter.
- Kindness can change the world.

Can you think of other reasons why kindness is important?

_____

_____

_____

_____

Practicing kindness starts with being kind to ourselves.
Imagine that you have a kindness piggy bank inside of you,
you need to fill it up first by being kind to yourself
and taking care of your needs.

When your bank is full, it is easier to share your time
and energy and be kind to others from a place of joy.

Inside this piggy bank, we put in
kind intentions, kind thoughts,
kind words and kind deeds.

In some of the illustrations of the book, our little rabbits are practicing kindness in different ways. Look at the images below and discuss what they may be doing that shows kindness.

Create your own story using one of these illustrations as a starting point.

Create your own drawing of different acts of kindness being practiced.

There are many different ways to practice kindness. Everyone can be kind and do something nice for someone else.

Here are some suggestions:

1. Say something nice to someone.
2. Spend time outside appreciating nature.
3. Bake something for a friend or neighbor.
4. Plant something in your garden.
5. Make someone smile.
6. Spend time with an elderly person.
7. Donate to your local food bank.
8. Play a game with a sibling or a friend.
9. Help cook a meal for your family.
10. Share your books.
11. Let someone else go first.
12. Pick up litter.
13. Share a joke.
14. Be friendly with someone new.
15. Help someone finish a project.
16. Hold the door open for someone.
17. Give someone a flower or small gift.
18. Volunteer your time to help out.
19. Write a nice letter.
20. Give a hug.
21. Take care of your pets.
22. Draw a picture for someone.
23. Say thank you.
24. Share a nice story.
25. Help make a meal.
26. Read to someone.
27. Teach someone something new.
28. Share your passion.
29. Help a neighbor.
30. Make a get well card for someone.

Can you share your ideas?

_____

_____

_____

_____

_____

_____

_____

_____

_____

_____

_____

_____

Practicing gratitude is a way to practice kindness by focusing on the good that surrounds us and acknowledging it.

We can practice gratitude by:

- Telling someone we are grateful for them
- Noticing and sharing what we are grateful for
- Counting our blessings by writing down
  1-3 things that we are grateful for
- Sharing the joy of our gratitude with others

Can you think of people, experiences, moments, or things that you are grateful for?

Thank you for being a kind friend!

_____

_____

_____

_____

_____

_____

_____

_____

_____

_____

How can you and your family practice kindness? Draw your ideas here.

Books, journals, activity sheets, encouragement tools, support material and more...

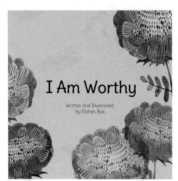

www.plantlovegrow.com

For free printable pages related to this book:
www.plantlovegrow.com/measure-your-day-in-kindness
www.plantlovegrow.com/virtues

Manufactured by Amazon.ca
Bolton, ON